The Hunter

A Chinese Folktale

retold by

Mary Casanova

illustrations by

Ed Young

Atheneum Books for Young Readers

New York London Toronto Sydney Singapore

The author first heard this story from an exchange student from Chang Chun, the capital city in the Ji Lin province of northeast China. The tale that was shared may be found in *Zhongguo Tonghua (Chinese Fairy Tales)* under the title *Lieh Ren Hai Li Bu (The Hunter Hai Li Bu)*, edited by Zheng Shuo Ren and Gu Nai Qing and published by Shang Hai Wen Yi.

Suffer
Drought

Magic
Rock

Heavenly
Secret (Plan)

Snatch
Soar

All
Benefit

Turning to
Stone

Hasten
Rescue

Flood
Disaster

Downpour

Dragon
Palace

Begging to
Escape

Buried

Reward with
Treasure

Doubt
All

Trust

Atheneum Books for Young Readers An imprint of Simon & Schuster Children's Publishing Division 1230 Avenue of the Americas New York, New York 10020 Text copyright © 2000 by Mary Casanova Illustrations copyright © 2000 by Ed Young All rights reserved including the right of reproduction in whole or in part in any form. Book design by Michael Nelson The text of this book is set in Papyrus ICG. The illustrations are rendered in pastel and gouache. Printed in Hong Kong
2   4   6   8   10   9   7   5   3   1
Library of Congress Cataloging-in-Publication Data Casanova, Mary. The hunter: a Chinese folktale /retold by Mary Casanova; illustrations by Ed Young. p. cm. Summary: After learning to understand the language of animals, Hai Li Bu the hunter sacrifices himself to save his village. ISBN 0-689-82906-X (alk. paper) [1. Folklore—China.] I. Young, Ed, ill. II. Title. PZ8.1.C22783Hu 2000 398.2'0951'02—dc21 [E] 99-32166

FIRST
EDITION

To my dear friend,
Wu Geng Hui,
who first shared
this story
with my family.
—M. C.

For
Eugene Winick
—E. Y.

ONCE, IN A TINY CHINESE VILLAGE
wedged between mountains and sea, lived
a young hunter named Hai Li Bu. Though
Hai Li Bu was a good hunter, providing
fresh fish and meat for the villagers as best
he could, a drought came. Day after dry
day, the sun scorched the countryside and
burned the villagers' crops. Soon there
wasn't enough food to go around. The
children rarely laughed, the young women
seldom sang, and the white-haired people
were too weak to leave their mats. Worst
of all, the villagers began to argue and
stopped listening to one another.

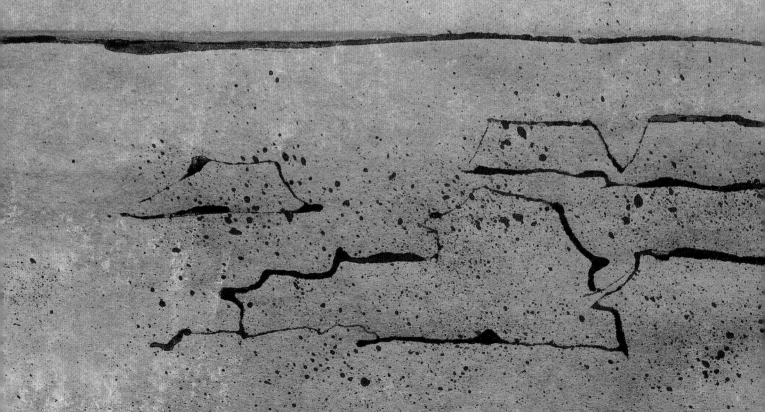

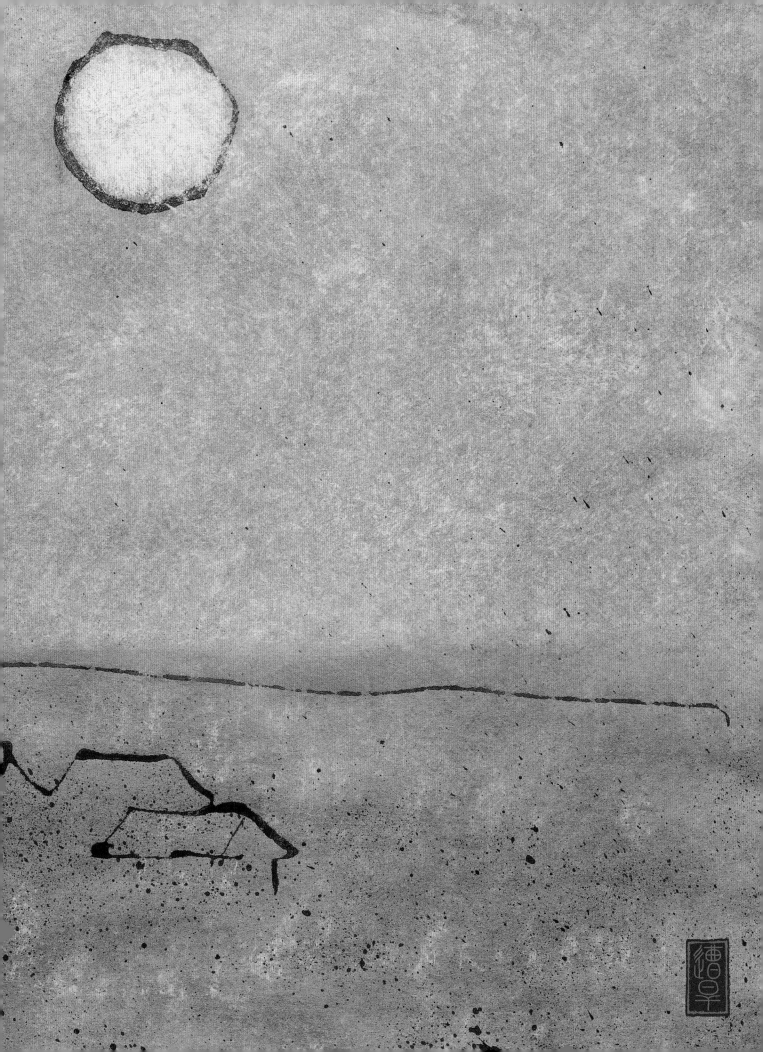

With each passing day, Hai Li Bu
hunted deeper and deeper in the forest,
desperately searching for game. One day, he
spotted a small, pearly snake warming itself on a rock.
Not wanting to disturb the snake's sleep, Hai Li Bu
stepped softly around it on the withered grass.

Suddenly,
a crane dropped from
the clouds. Flapping its long
gray wings, it snatched up the pearly
snake and climbed high into the sky.
   "Help me!" the little snake cried.
   What? thought Hai Li Bu. The snake
can speak?

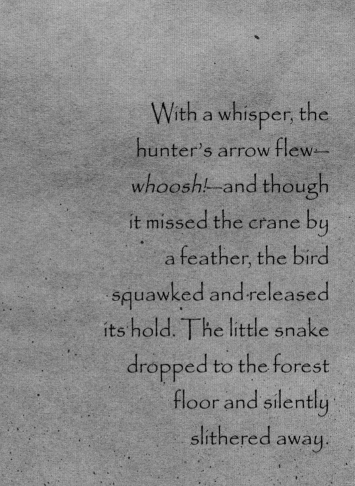

With a whisper, the
hunter's arrow flew—
whoosh!—and though
it missed the crane by
a feather, the bird
squawked and released
its hold. The little snake
dropped to the forest
floor and silently
slithered away.

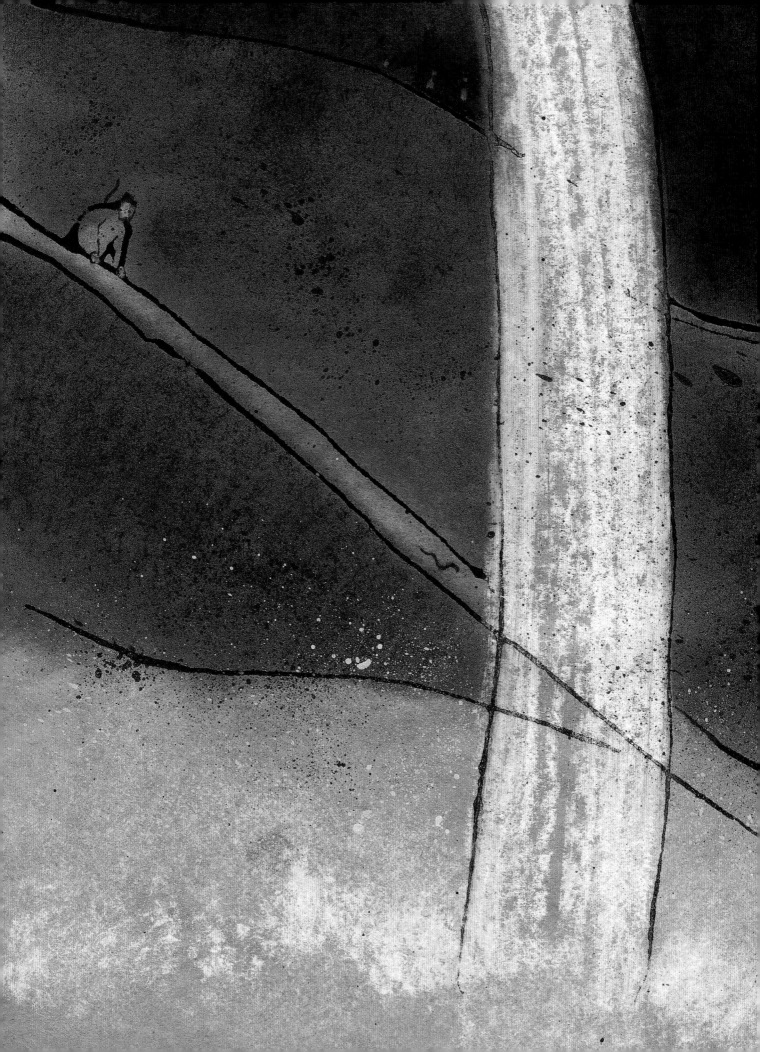

The next day, when Hai Li Bu returned to the forest, the little snake approached him on the path.

"My father, the Dragon King of the Sea," she said, "wants to thank you for saving my life. Will you come?"

Though Hai Li Bu needed to hunt, he didn't want to offend the snake. "Of course," he replied, and followed her down a winding path to a crystal palace beneath the sea.

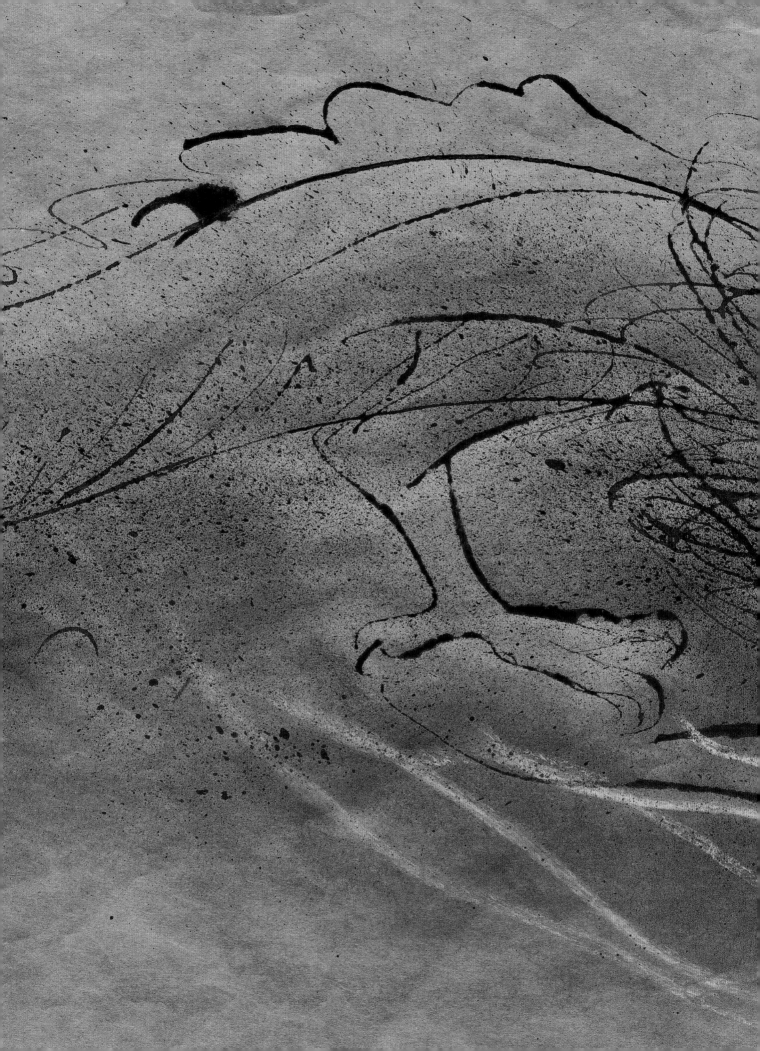

From his throne, the Dragon King asked, "What do you want for saving my daughter?"

Hai Li Bu shrugged his broad shoulders. "What more could I need, except to better provide for my village?"

The Dragon King showed Hai Li Bu his thousand and seventy treasures: sparkling red rubies, forest green emeralds, ocean blue sapphires, and shimmery pink pearls. "I will give you anything," he said.

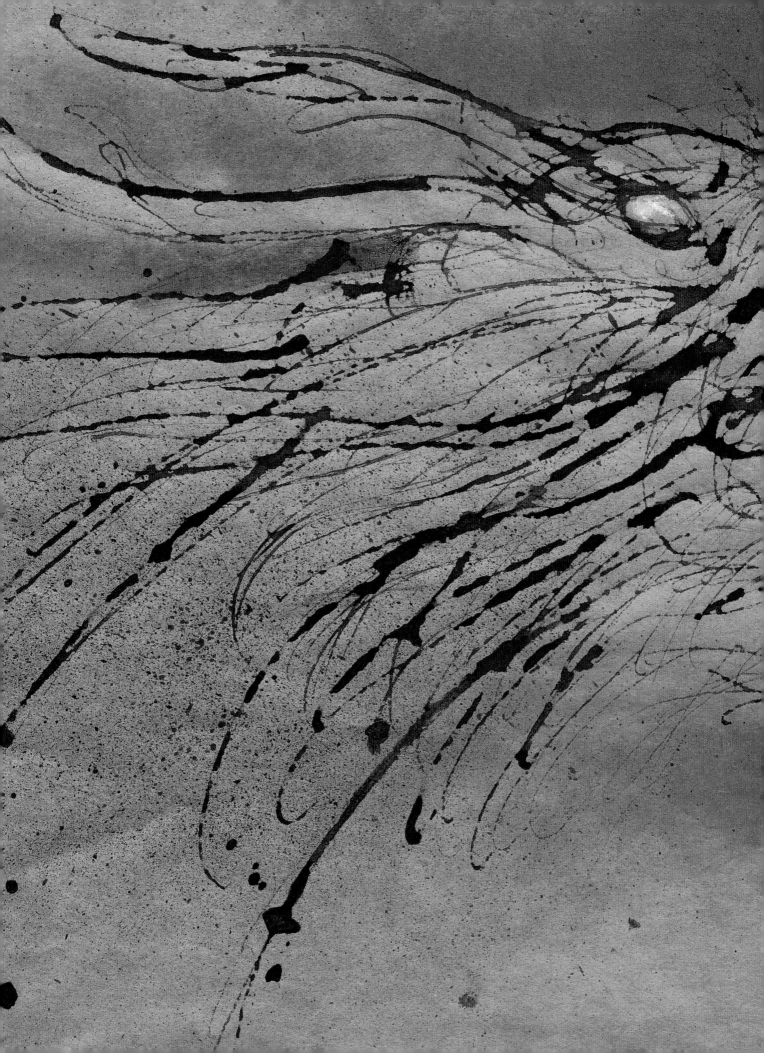

"Your treasures are
beautiful," the hunter answered,
"but the only thing I desire is to understand
the language of animals. Then I can be a better hunter."
The Dragon King reared back and from out of his mouth shot a round
stone. "Take it," he said, "and your wish will come true. But remember
one thing: You must not pass on the secret of your gift, or you will
surely turn to stone, like the one you now hold."

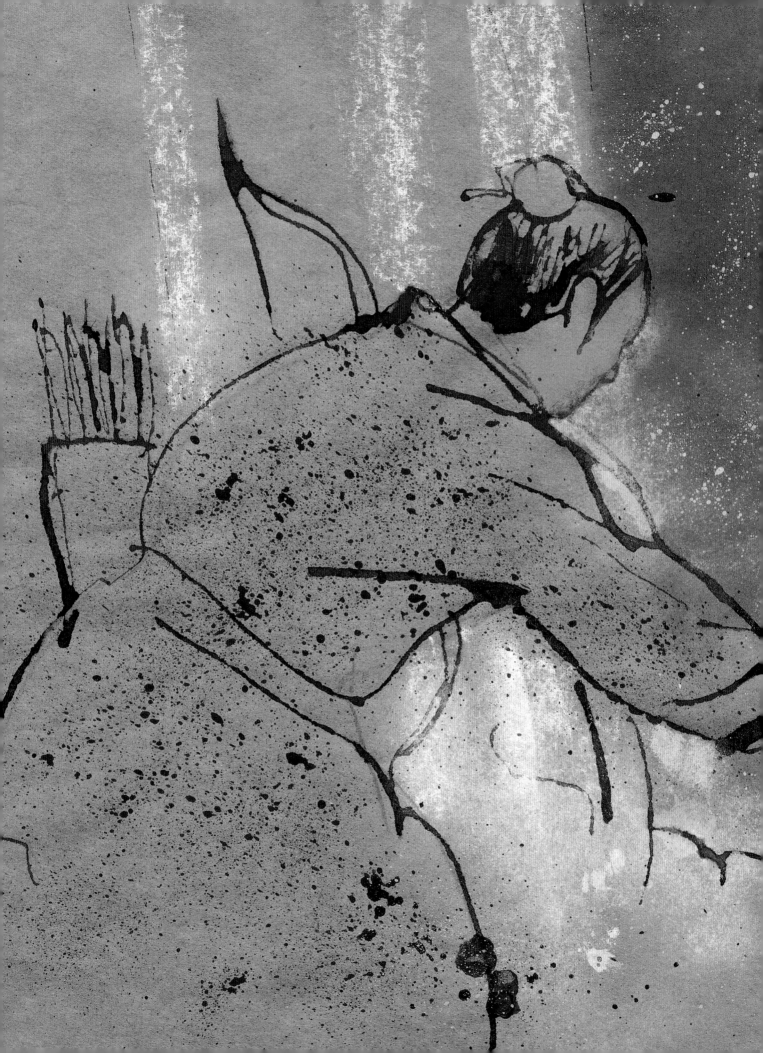

With the stone in his leather pouch, Hai Li Bu hurried back to the forest. From the chatter of finches he learned where mountain goats wandered and where wild boar bedded down. He learned of shallows where fish were plentiful and where clams clustered in the sand. Each day, Hai Li Bu returned to his parched village with an even greater offering of food. Soon, the village was filled with laughter. The children's cheeks grew round and soft. The white-haired people left their mats to share their stories. The young women sang songs and whispered about who Hai Li Bu would someday marry.

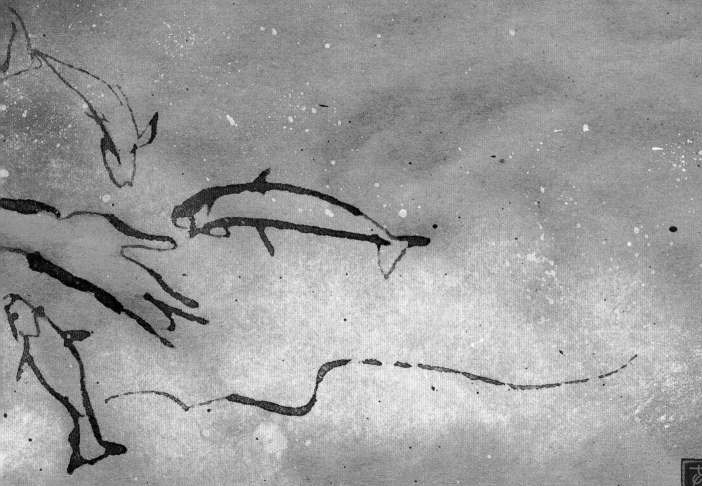

But one dawn, the forest was unusually full with the chatter of birds and animals.

"Lightning and heavy rains are coming," cried the foxes. "The entire village will be flooded!"

"Tomorrow," the bears bellowed, "the mountaintop will crumble to the sea!"

"Who knows," the birds called, "how many people will die!"

Hai Li Bu's mouth went dry as the drought. He dropped his bow to the ground and rushed back to his village to warn his people.

"Listen!" he shouted. "We must leave! The village will be destroyed!"

The villagers gathered around him, looking sideways at Hai Li Bu.

"Maybe he's been in the woods too long," said a young woman.

"Maybe he needs a rest," said a white-haired man.

"Maybe he's joking," said a child.

"Please," begged Hai Li Bu, "you must listen and believe me!"

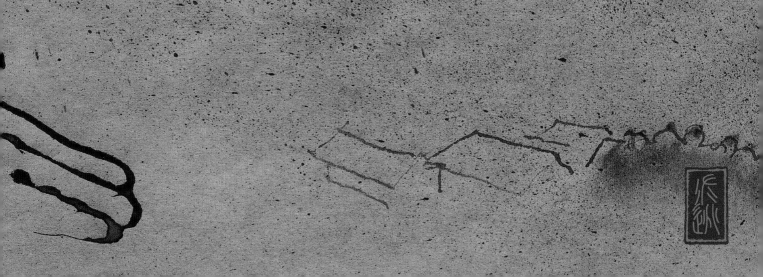

A village elder stepped forward. "Where did you learn this terrible news?"
Hai Li Bu suddenly remembered the Dragon King's warning.
He whispered, "Do you want me to die so you can believe?"
"Of course not," the elder said. He squared his
arms and gestured to the simple huts. "But
you ask us to leave our homes. How
can we know what you say is true?"

Hai Li Bu stroked his chin. What should he do? If they wouldn't listen, should he flee and save himself? The villagers pressed closer. Like the wind that began to stir the treetops, they whispered among themselves.

How could he make them listen? He reached into his pouch and in his palm held out the round, luminous stone. But the villagers looked blankly at the stone and at Hai Li Bu.

The hunter sighed. He studied the villagers' faces—young and old—more splendid than jewels. No. Of course he could never allow them to be destroyed.

Raindrops began to fall—*plink, plink, plink*—on the dusty street.

Hai Li Bu drew a deep breath. He told of the little snake and the Dragon King's gift. Then he pointed to the inky line of birds flying south. "Look," he said, "the birds flee." As he spoke, his toes grew stiff as stones. "Tomorrow the mountain will be struck by lightning," he added, and his legs became granite hard. "The village will be flooded," he said, and his hands stopped in midair. "Listen," he said, "believe me and have courage." And as he spoke these last words, his lips turned to stone.

The villagers were stunned. They threw themselves at Hai Li Bu's feet and wept. As the rain grew heavier, the villagers ran to their houses, packed what they could carry on their backs, and fled.

The next day, as the animals had warned, thunder rattled the countryside. Lightning cracked the mountain peak, and boulders crashed into the valley below. Raindrops fell in sheets and washed the valley, utterly destroying the tiny village.

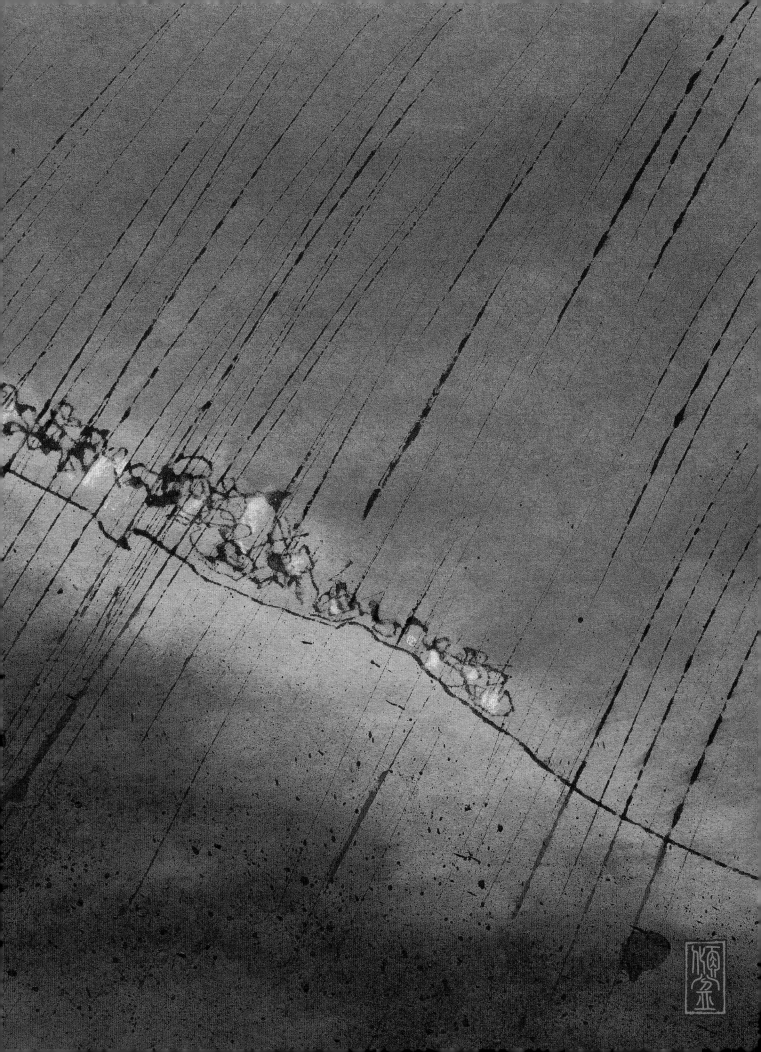

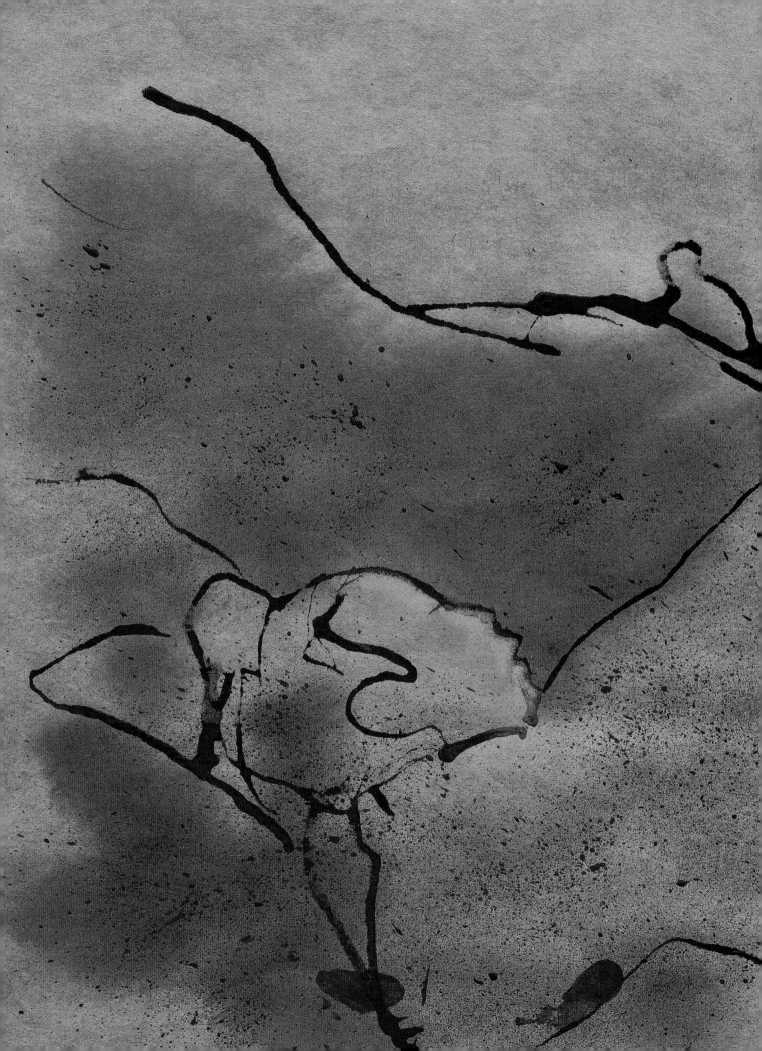

Days passed, and the people returned. But before rebuilding their village, they searched for Hai Li Bu in his stone prison. They found him, half-buried in the mud, and gently, gently, with many hands and many tears, carried him to what remained of the top of the mountain. "If only we had not doubted him," the people said. "If only we'd listened."

And to this day it is said that somewhere in
China, high on a mountain peak, still stands
the statue of Hai Li Bu, gazing upon
his valley below, where the
villagers listen to every
person, including the
youngest child.

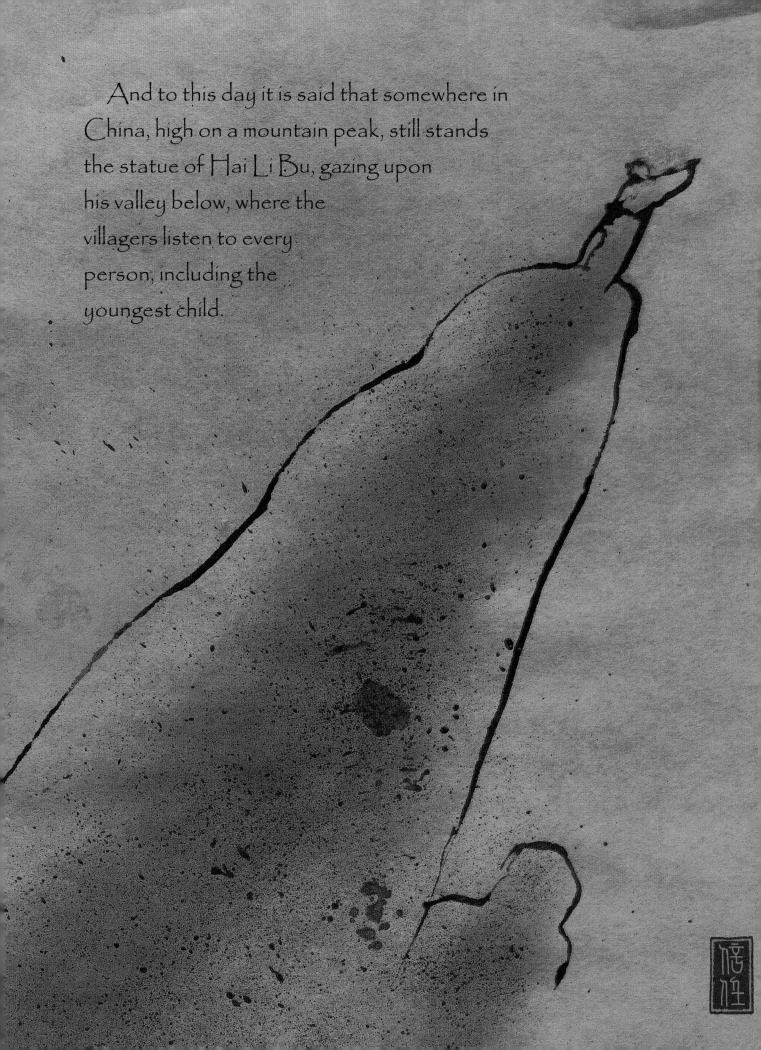